This book belongs to:

_____

_____

_____

First published 2014 by Walker Books Ltd
87 Vauxhall Walk, London SE11 5HJ

2 4 6 8 10 9 7 5 3 1

© 2014 Lucy Cousins
Lucy Cousins font © 2014 Lucy Cousins

The author/illustrator has asserted her moral rights

Illustrated in the style of Lucy Cousins by King Rollo Films Ltd

Maisy™. Maisy is a registered trademark of Walker Books Ltd, London

Printed in China

British Library Cataloguing in Publication Data:
a catalogue record for this book is
available from the British Library.

ISBN 978-1-4063-4954-2

www.walker.co.uk

Maisy Goes to the Cinema

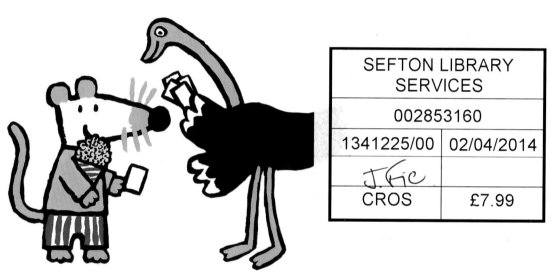

Lucy Cousins

WALKER BOOKS
AND SUBSIDIARIES
LONDON • BOSTON • SYDNEY • AUCKLAND

Today, Maisy and her friends
are going to the cinema.
"Oh, I am **SO** excited!" says Tallulah.
"Can we buy popcorn?" asks Charley.
"I **LOVE** popcorn!"

There are lots and lots of different films showing. What will they go and see?

Dusty Rider

Maisy buys five tickets for "Hero in the Jungle" and some SNACKS!

Popcorn, a big drink, frozen yoghurt and ice cream — YUM!

Ev ryone likes adv nture movies and Troy T. Tiger (a very BIG movie star) is starring in this one.

Wow! It's a BIG screen! Tallulah wants to sit in the middle and Cyril wants to sit next to Maisy.

Eddie and Charley want to sit at the very front!

The movie starts and the lights go down slowly...

Cyril doesn't like the dark cinema. "Don't worry, Cyril," says Maisy. "You can hold my hand."

"That's my favourite movie star!"
shouts Eddie when Troy T. Tiger
appears on screen.

Charley laughs so much that he spills all his popcorn on the floor!

It's nearly half way through the film now and Tallulah needs the toilet.

"Me too," says Cyril.

"Me three!" says Eddie.

So they go as fast as they can.

And wash their hands very quickly.

"Hurry! Hurry!" says Eddie. They don't want to miss anything.

There's one very scary part when Troy T. Tiger meets a big, huge ... DINOSAUR!

"I can't watch!" says Cyril,
and he hides behind his hands.

Phew! It's a happy ending! Eddie shouts, "I LOVE TROY T. TIGER FOREVER!"

Afterwards, Maisy
and her friends all talk
about their favourite
part of the film.

"What will we do now?" says Cyril.
"I know," says
Eddie...

"Let's go to see 'Hero in the Jungle' ... AGAIN!"